TRUCKS THAT BUILD

To Mark and Stephanie

First Aladdin Paperbacks Edition, May 1999

Text and photographs copyright © 1999 by Lars Klove

Aladdin Paperbacks
An imprint of Simon & Schuster Children's Publishing Division
1230 Avenue of the Americas
New York, NY 10020

READY-TO-READ is a registered trademark of Simon & Schuster, Inc.
Also available in a Simon & Schuster Books for Young Readers hardcover edition.

The text for this book was set in Utopia.

Printed and bound in the United States of America

10 9 8 7 6 5 4 3 2 1

The Library of Congress has cataloged
'the Simon & Schuster Books for Young Readers edition as follows:
Klove, Lars.
Trucks that build / written and illustrated by Lars Klove.
p.   cm. — (Ready-to-read)
Summary: A simple description of various trucks that work to build,
including a tree chopper, backhoe, and bulldozer.
ISBN 0-689-81762-2 (hc.)
1. Trucks—Juvenile literature. 2. Earthmoving machinery—Juvenile literature.
3. Building—Juvenile literature.
[1. Trucks. 2. Earthmoving machinery. 3. Building.] I. Title. II. Series.
TL230.15.K58   1999
629.225—dc21   98-36616
CIP   AC
ISBN 0-689-81761-4 (pbk.)

TRUCKS THAT BUILD

Written and illustrated by Lars Klove

READY-TO-READ

Aladdin Paperbacks

TO THE READER:

One of the good things about learning to read is finding out about things that interest you. Do you like trucks? Here is a book that shows you many different kinds of trucks and what they can do.

Sometimes when you read, you can almost feel as if you are really there. Want to hear the sound of the beeping when a truck backs up? Want to feel the ground shake when the roller is spreading dirt? Put on your hard hat and begin to read!

The town is building a school.

Workers are hired who can build the school.

They bring their trucks.

They are ready to start.

There is a *beep, beep* sound when a truck backs up. Pay attention!

The land is covered with trees.

Some of the trees must be cut down.

A road must be built.

The **TREE CHOPPER** has a sharp clipper on its front that can grab a tree trunk.

TREE CHOPPER

SKIDDER

LOG TRUCK

8

A **SKIDDER** pulls logs to the log truck.

The **LOG TRUCK** brings the biggest logs to the lumber mill.

A **CHIPPER** chops up branches and leaves.

CHIPPER

A **BACKHOE** pulls stumps out of the ground and clears away dirt.

BACKHOE

A **SAND TRUCK** brings sand to the building site.

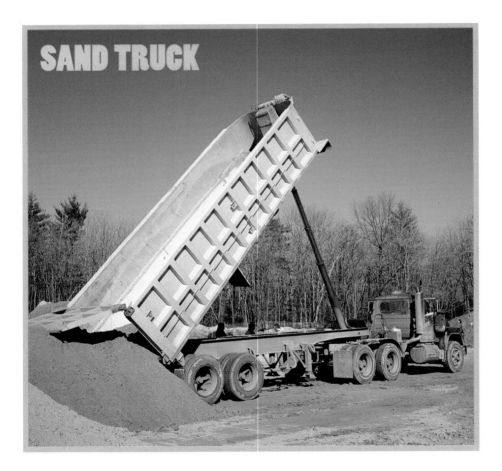

SAND TRUCK

A **FRONT LOADER** can also help.

FRONT LOADER

Then the **BULLDOZER** puts dirt on
the building site.

The ground must be completely flat.

Then a **ROLLER** packs the sand down flat.

The roller vibrates.
You can feel it in your feet!

The EXCAVATOR
digs trenches in the ground.

Now the **CONCRETE TRUCK**
pours the foundation.

The workers must clean the truck every time they use it, or the concrete will harden.

One day a man in
a **GASOLINE TRUCK** stopped by.

Can you guess what he did?

The backhoe digs a new trench on the site.

The trenches will hold the pipes that bring water or electrical wires into the school.

If there are rocks too large for the backhoe, they are broken up by the **HOBKNOCKER**.

Now the school walls can be built.

A **FLATBED TRUCK** brings
steel beams and columns
to the building site.

A **CRANE** lifts them into place.

CRANE

A **LIFT** brings bricks and mortar up to the workers.

A large **DUMP TRUCK**, filled with hot asphalt, works with a **SPREADER**.

A roller packs down the surface
to make it strong.

The school is finished.

All the trucks leave.

Their work is done.